Horse Show!
A Donkey-Donk Story

Ellen F. Feld
Photographed by John Cebula

To My Brother Bill
For Always Being There

I would like to thank members of the Hampshire County Riding Club for volunteering to bring their horses to Donk's horse show. In addition, a huge thank you to John Cebula for his amazing patience during our photo shoots for *Horse Show!*

Visit www.willowbendpublishing.com to discover more horse books for children of all ages.

Copyright © 2019 by Ellen F. Feld

Published by Willow Bend Publishing

Library of Congress Catalog Card Number: 2019902162

ISBN: 978-1-7337674-0-8

Direct inquiries to: Willow Bend Publishing
P.O. Box 304
Goshen, MA 01032
www.willowbendpublishing.com

Photography by John Cebula
Book design by Creative Publishing Design

Printed in USA

My name is Donkey-Donk. You can call me Donk. I am a miniature donkey.

I'm going to a horse show!
Maybe I will win a blue ribbon.

At the horse show, I'm going to go in a trail class. In the trail class, I will have to go over, under, or through different obstacles.

Over

Under

Through

I wonder what obstacles will be at the show. I might have to go over a jump. I better practice...

Ta-Da! Now I can jump!

I might have to open a gate.
I better practice…

Ta-Da! Now I can open a gate!

I might have to walk around cones.
I better practice...

Ta-Da! Now I can walk around cones.

Before I go to the show, I need a bath. Rub-a-dub-dub, I'm a donkey in a tub!

Now it's time to go to the show.

Wow! There are a lot of horses here.

First, I have to go through a hoop.
I think I'm stuck.

Next, I have to go under some ribbons. That tickles.

One last obstacle – a podium.
I think I can do this!

Ta-da!

And the winner is…
Donkey-Donk!